THIS WALKER BOOK BELONGS TO:

_____

_____

_____

_____

For Alice and Melissa (Laura)

First published 1992
by Walker Books Ltd
87 Vauxhall Walk
London SE11 5HJ

This edition published 1999

2 4 6 8 10 9 7 5 3 1

© 1992 Penny Dale

This book has been typeset in Veronan Light Educational.

Printed in Hong Kong/China

British Library Cataloguing in Publication Data
A catalogue record for this book is
available from the British Library.

ISBN 0-7445-6937-0

ALL ABOUT
Alice

PENNY DALE

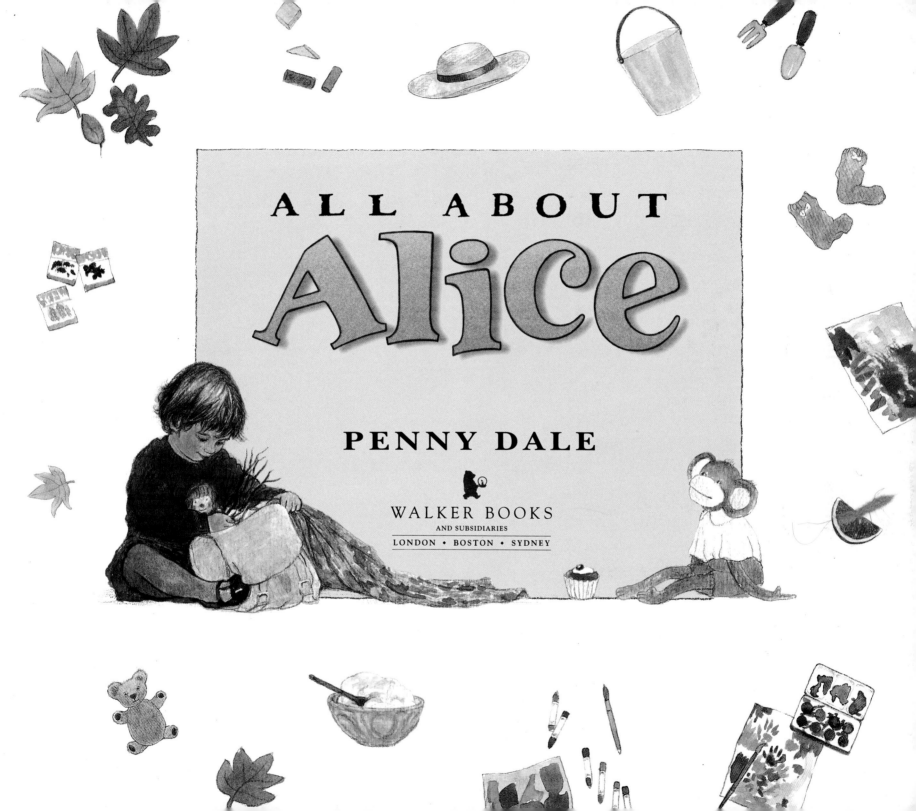

WALKER BOOKS
AND SUBSIDIARIES
LONDON · BOSTON · SYDNEY

Alice was getting dressed. So was her big sister Laura.

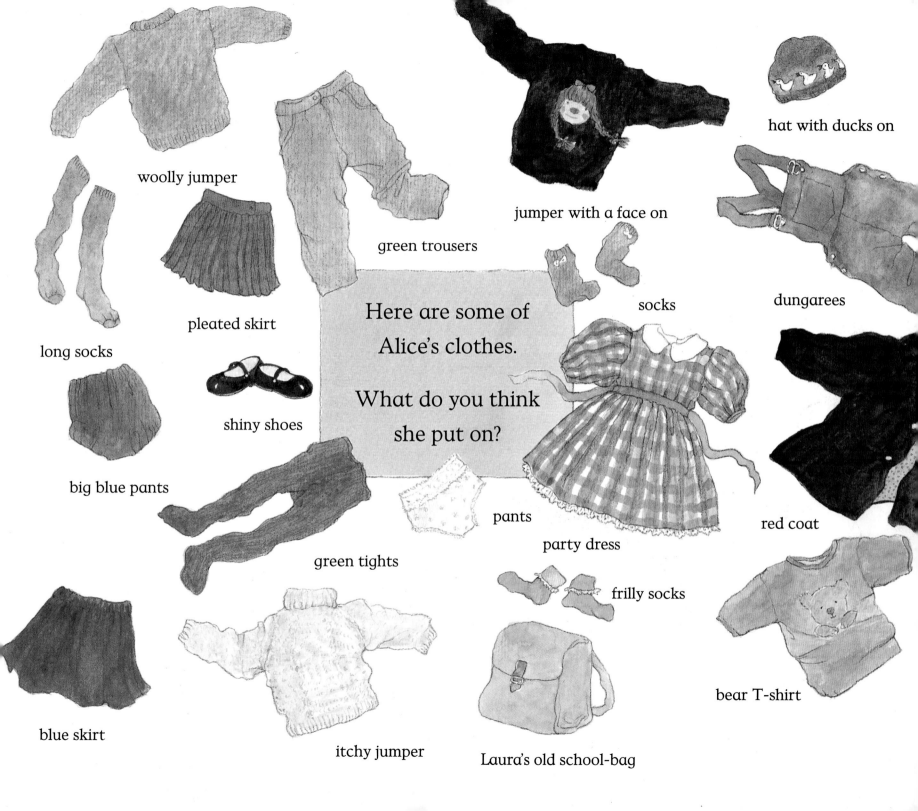

woolly jumper

hat with ducks on

jumper with a face on

green trousers

socks

dungarees

long socks

pleated skirt

Here are some of Alice's clothes.

What do you think she put on?

shiny shoes

big blue pants

pants

red coat

green tights

party dress

frilly socks

blue skirt

itchy jumper

Laura's old school-bag

bear T-shirt

Alice put on her jumper with a face on, her green trousers, her blue skirt, her hat with ducks, and Laura's old school-bag.

Then Dad came in and helped her dress properly and took her down to breakfast.

apple

milk

bread and jam

cheese

raisins

egg with soldiers

What do you think
Alice had for breakfast?

banana

toast

raisins

orange

cereal

yoghurt

biscuits

Alice had cereal for breakfast, but she didn't eat it.
Alice wanted her sister's breakfast.

drink

recorder and music

badge

pencil-case

hanky

lunch-box

reading book

folder

After breakfast Laura packed her school-bag. This is what she put in it.

crayons

old raisins

leaves

Laura's cake

scrumpled
paper

scarf

Alice packed her
school-bag too.

What do you think
she put in it?

car

jewels

pink recorder

crusts

monkey

bits of
cereal

book

lump of coal

twigs

old sweet

Alice put everything in her school-bag, except her monkey and her sister's cake.

She carried her monkey and gave back the cake.

Mum, Alice and Laura walked to school.

In the playground Alice started crying. Why do you think Alice cried?

Alice cried because the big children went into school without her.

She was too young to go to school.

Mum and Alice walked home.

driving the tractor

playing in the garden

reading

making a house

playing school

playing with bricks

These are some things which Alice likes doing at home.

When she got home, what do you think Alice did?

painting

helping with the dishes

cooking

At home Alice went straight upstairs to play school.

She went out in the garden and found a spider.

She did some painting and cooking and reading. She helped with the dishes.

one small tomato

three pieces of cheese

two sandwiches

twenty-seven crisps

half a yoghurt

four slices of cucumber

one big apple

her cake like Laura's

At lunch-time Alice had a picnic in the garden. This is what she ate.

After lunch Alice made a house and drove the tractor round the garden.

She went back upstairs to play school, and then it was time for a rest.

bird

rabbit

koala

mouse

Who do you think
Alice had a rest with?

little ted

big ted

monkey

fox

Alice rested with all the animals.

Mum woke Alice when it was time to fetch Laura from school. Alice was cross at first.

But soon she was smiling again. Why do you think she was smiling?

Alice was smiling because she knew the big children were about to come out of school.

After school Alice played with Amy and the twins. Then it was time to go home.

Can you see Laura?

What do you think Alice did all the way home?

All the way home Alice copied her sister.

When they got home Alice went on copying her sister.
She copied her playing the recorder. She copied her watching TV.

She copied her going upstairs. What do you think happened
when Laura went into their room?

When Laura went into their room, she was cross with Alice because of the mess.
She said she wanted to play on her own and collected up her things.

Alice played on her own too. But she didn't collect up her things, she got more out.

tie-on wings

dressing-up clothes

old decorations

Here are the things
Alice got out.

What do you think
happened next?

masks

face paints

hats

Alice got dressed up. Then the twins and Amy came round.

Everyone got dressed up like Alice . . .

and ran out into the garden to play.

MORE WALKER PAPERBACKS
For You to Enjoy

Also by Penny Dale

TEN IN THE BED

"A subtle variation on the traditional nursery song,
illustrated with wonderfully warm pictures ...
crammed with amusing details." *Practical Parenting*

0-7445-1340-5   £4.99

TEN OUT OF BED

"A counting backwards version of *Ten in the Bed* ... Penny Dale's warm and
distinctive illustrations are full of action and movement ...
lots to look at, smile at and talk about." *Children's Books of the Year*

0-7445-4383-5   £4.99

BET YOU CAN'T!

"A lively argumentative dialogue – using simple,
repetitive words – between two children. Illustrated with
great humour and realism." *Practical Parenting*

0-7445-1225-5   £4.99

Walker Paperbacks are available from most booksellers, or by post from B.B.C.S., P.O. Box 941, Hull, North Humberside HU1 3YQ

24 hour telephone credit card line 01482 224626

To order, send: Title, author, ISBN number and price for each book ordered, your full name and address,
cheque or postal order payable to BBCS for the total amount and allow the following for postage and packing:
UK and BFPO: £1.00 for the first book, and 50p for each additional book to a maximum of £3.50.
Overseas and Eire: £2.00 for the first book, £1.00 for the second and 50p for each additional book.
Prices and availability are subject to change without notice.